A Bride for Karl

Book Six
Brides of Broken Arrow

Cheryl Wright

A BRIDE FOR KARL
Book Six
Brides of Broken Arrow

Copyright ©2022 by Cheryl Wright

Cover Artist: Black Widow Books

Editing: Amber Downey

Dedication

To Margaret Tanner, my very dear friend and fellow author, for her enduring encouragement and friendship.

To Alan, my husband of over forty-eight years, who has been a relentless supporter of my writing and dreams for many years.

To Virginia McKevitt, cover artist and friend, who always creates the most amazing covers for my books.

To You, my wonderful readers, who encourage me to continue writing these stories. It is such a joy knowing so many of you enjoy reading my stories as much as I love writing them for you.

In Memory

In memory of my dear great-aunt Florrie, who lived in a small town in the middle of nowhere. She was a tough old bird, and definitely rough around the edges, but had a heart of gold.

Following her lead, I've never let and never will let, any male (young or old) sit at my table without a shirt, or any bare chest showing.

Table of Contents

Chapter One

Karl Adams loved nothing more than playing with his young nephew, Clyde, Floyd and Kathryn's son in his spare time. It did, however, send a blast of need through him. As much as he longed for a wife and child, he'd been reluctant to send for a proxy bride.

At least until now.

He glanced up in time to see his brother Floyd pull his wife to him. Another pang of want wracked him. No matter how much Floyd had tried to convince him to send away for a proxy bride, Karl had resisted. He didn't see the need for it, and certainly didn't want to be accountable to another person.

Perhaps it was time to rethink his stance. He had seen how happy Floyd had been since he'd married, and wanted that for himself as well. Why it had taken so long for him to come to that conclusion, Karl did not know. Being the last single male on Jacob's part of the ranch may have something to do with it, but he really wasn't certain. He only knew it was at the back of his mind often.

Kathryn left the room momentarily, and when she returned handed him an envelope addressed to Karl, care of Floyd. He stared at the envelope for what seemed to be minutes, but in reality was only seconds. *Why would anyone send him a letter via his brother?* It was the strangest thing.

"This is for you," Kathryn said quietly, which seemed out of character for his sister-in-law. "I hope you don't mind," she said, then licked her lips. Floyd said nothing, but pulled her close.

Karl glanced from one to the other of them. Something was up, but he had no idea what that could be. Turning the envelope over, he noted the details on the back.

Florence Reeves

Care of Post Office

Clear Valley, Idaho

That was strange. He didn't know anyone in Idaho, and he sure didn't know this Florence Reeves. He carefully opened the envelope, ensuring he didn't rip the contents. The folded paper was heavily perfumed. Even more weird.

When he looked up, his every move was being monitored. *What did they do?* He already felt his brother and sister-in-law had set him up, and not in the nicest way, either. He stared pointedly at the pair. "This is your doing, isn't it, Floyd?" He knew in his heart it was his brother. Kathryn wasn't the type to go behind someone's back. Well, normally, neither was Floyd, but he'd been persistent lately that his brother needed a bride.

Karl was about to screw up the unopened letter and throw it in the trash when he remembered the unknown sender. Florence Reeves was also an innocent victim in all of this. He at least owed her the opportunity to have her story read. He sighed loudly and unfolded the fragrant paper.

Dear Karl,

I hope you don't mind if I call you by your first name. After all, in our marriage, I would not go about calling you Mr. Adams.

Karl couldn't help but chuckle. He already like this Florence person.

I guess I should tell you some more about myself. You already know I'm a spinster of twenty-eight years. I am about average height at 5'5" and have long red hair. According to my father, I have fiery red hair with a temperament to match.

Well, that's just great. A wife with a temper—just what he needed.

Karl was ready to screw the paper up, but as he closed his hand around the flimsy paper, the remaining words swam in front of his eyes.

The reason I'm writing is to let you know I'll be arriving by stagecoach...

He read and reread the date. This woman who was previously unknown to him was arriving the next morning! His head shot up and he glared at Floyd. "You told her I'd marry her?" Anger flooded him and he stood, ready to leave, his entire body tense. "I don't even know this woman. It's quite obvious, though, that you have corresponded with her for some time."

"I..." Floyd was lost for words for once.

"What am I to do now? I suppose she probably thinks it was me corresponding with her? That is low, brother." He clenched his fists. Karl was not a violent man, yet had to resist the urge to slap his older brother.

"It was me," Kathryn whispered, but Karl knew that wasn't true. Knowing his sister-in-law, she was trying to keep the peace. Making sure a rift didn't develop between the brothers.

He stormed out of the cottage, his mind in confusion. The woman was arriving the next morning, and he did not know if he would marry her. Or even wanted to marry her. Suddenly he skidded to a halt, then turned back, his heart pounding. "Tell me we're not already married," he demanded.

Floyd didn't say a word, he didn't have to. Karl could see from his brother's expression the woman already on her way to Halliwell was his legal wife. His proxy bride.

The damage was done, and there was little he could do about it except arrange for an annulment. But where did that leave Florence Reeves? There must be a reason she was willing to marry a complete stranger, sight unseen.

Florence stared out the stagecoach window. She'd had enough of traveling and couldn't wait to arrive in Halliwell. Karl Adams sounded like a good person, a clean-living Christian man who was also a hard worker.

She had always admired cowboys. Well, if she was truthful, as a young girl she had fantasized about marrying a cowboy. She had no idea why, except she'd seen them riding their horses and thought that seemed appealing. Of course, it would be to a pre-teen; now she wasn't so sure. From what she'd learned, it could be a pretty dirty and even dangerous job.

Besides, the cowboys her father hired were far from gentlemen. Of the few men her father hired, most of them were drunks. And her father... she didn't even want to think about him. She'd escaped without interference, and that was the main thing.

She was impatient to arrive and meet her husband. It seemed like she'd been traveling for days without a break, which was totally untrue. They'd stopped at least twice a day for meal breaks and, sometimes, for the horses to be changed over. The food at the stage depots was pretty ordinary, but better than not eating at all.

Florence couldn't wait to get to Karl's cottage and back to some home cooking. Assuming that was, he had stores. She was well aware of the habits of cowboys, since one quite repulsive cowboy had pursued her relentlessly. She knew he was not necessarily the norm and hoped fervently that her new husband did not fall into the same category.

She shook herself mentally. If she'd believed that, she would never have agreed to their proxy marriage.

She glanced outside as the horses slowed. Were they finally in Halliwell, or was this simply yet another stop along the way? She breathed a sigh of relief when she noticed the sign that identified this town as her destination. It didn't appear to be a large town, not that she expected it to be. There were a handful of stores that she could see from her point of vision and hoped there were even more. The last thing she wanted was to have to travel long distances to carry out her regular shopping.

She was the only remaining passenger—the others had disembarked at their last stop a little over an hour ago. The driver opened the door and set down steps, and Florence began her descent into her new life.

Mrs. Karl Adams.

She was still getting used to her new name and title. Florence wondered what he would be like. She had a dreamy vision of him being the most handsome man in town. Not that she knew what her husband looked like, since they'd married in haste due to her situation. If her father had known what she had done, there would be consequences. Thankfully, he never found out.

As if out of her fantasies, a tall and incredibly handsome man stepped toward her. "Florence Adams?" Her heart fluttered. Standing in front of her was the man she'd married. He was well over six feet tall, and the most striking man she'd ever met.

She looked him up and down. He didn't appear much like a cowboy in his black suit, white shirt, and a tie that was perfect for church. Except for his cowboy hat, that was. The thought made her grin.

Florence finally found her tongue. "That's me. Are you my husband?" Her words sounded so fanciful that Florence bit her lip. Not in a million years did she ever believe she would marry a complete stranger.

He frowned then. "About that."

And here it comes. He'd sent her money for expenses, her ticket for the stagecoach, and even paid in advance for the hotels she needed to stay at along the way. Her shoulders slumped. *Should she climb back up those steps and go right back home again?* The thought was untenable.

On the verge of tears, she faced him head on. "You've changed your mind? I don't know what I'll do now." Her heart pounded and she couldn't think. Confusion totally overwhelmed her to the point Florence swayed and was suddenly held captive by two powerful hands.

He carefully lifted her off the ground and headed into the stage depot, where he sat her down. "The thing is," he said gently. "It was my brother who arranged this proxy marriage. I didn't know about this arrangement until last night."

Karl stared into her face. She had gone pale as the whitest snow. *Perhaps he should take to her to see Doc Petersen?* He was about to suggest it when her face softened. They were both in the same situation. What mattered now was what they did about it. "Do you need a doctor?" He had the best of intentions, but only wanted to do what she wanted. Excluding staying married, that was.

She shook her head, and her wavy auburn hair bounced about her face. "I'm fine, just in shock, I guess." She glanced down into her lap and studied her hands. "Why would your brother do such a thing?"

"He thought it was time I married. Been telling me so for months now. Probably longer." The color was slowly returning to her face, and Karl sighed with relief. "Shall we retire to the diner? You're probably hungry, and we can talk in private there," he said as he glanced about. The driver stood chatting to the depot clerk, and every word they uttered had the potential to be overheard.

"I am a little hungry," she said, tears still swimming in her eyes. "But since you don't intend to continue with this marriage, don't feel obligated."

His heart thudded. *Did she think him some sort of callous trickster?* He was far from that. They were both victims of Floyd's good intentions, but sometimes even the best objectives could go awry.

He stood up, towering over her. He didn't intend to scare her, but she looked terrified. *What had happened to this woman, his wife?*

He promptly sat down again.

"Let me take you to the diner. I promise you, I don't feel obligated to do anything." This time, he helped Florence to her feet as he stood. Her hands were soft and gentle, and he felt a buzz of something he didn't recognize as they were skin on skin. If it weren't for the fact she already seemed to resent him, he would have dropped her hand like a hot potato.

As she reached her full height, he watched as she stretched her spine and straightened her shoulders. *Was this his wife flexing her muscles, getting ready for a fight?* She said in her letter she had a temper. He inwardly groaned. *What had he let himself in for? Or should he say, what had his brother let him in for?*

Florence sat opposite him at the diner. She studied the menu far longer than he expected she would. At the back of his mind, he understood she was probably processing everything that had happened since she'd arrived.

She seemed nice enough and was certainly a beauty. Floyd couldn't have picked any better if he'd tried. But on second thought, Karl knew his brother would have initially contacted Teddy, the family solicitor, who would have made the arrangements. There must have been some uncertainty in Floyd's mind going by the few letters back and forth. They usually left it up to Teddy to make the final decision in proxy marriage cases, so what made this one different?

Karl was yet to find out, but he knew above all, Florence had to be desperate to marry him without once meeting the man she would live the rest of her life with. The thought softened his attitude somewhat, despite the fact he wanted to remain a bachelor.

"I had to get away," she suddenly blurted out, then stared at him for what seemed an eternity. She suddenly closed her eyes and a single tear ran down her cheek. It broke Karl's heart, and he reached across and wiped her tear away. Her skin was so soft and her statement made him feel more than a little protective toward her. "It wasn't life or death, but there were a few factors in play, which made my situation untenable." She glanced down into her lap and studied her hands again.

It was all he could do not to reach out and hold her hand.

"There were reasons that made it imperative I leave." She seemed reluctant to say more, and he had no intention of pushing her. She glanced into his face then, and licked her lips. His heart thudded. Karl couldn't understand why this tiny woman, this stranger, sitting opposite him was affecting him so much. He continued to study her, then suddenly she sighed. A deep, heartfelt sigh that cut right through to his heart.

She didn't say another word, and he had no thought to make her. One day, when she trusted him, perhaps she'd tell him. His heart thudded again. His plans with Florence didn't go beyond having a meal with her. *What made him think she would trust him in that short period?* "I apologize for all the inconvenience we have caused you." And he was. "I can put you up at the hotel until we decide our future." By that, he meant until Teddy could arrange an annulment and they could then go on about their separate lives.

Moments later, their waitress arrived to take their orders. Then she disappeared as quickly as she'd arrived. It wasn't long before their meals were placed in front of them. He watched as Florence ate. It was as though she hadn't eaten a decent meal for days. Karl suddenly realized that could be right— traveling on the stage didn't make it easy to eat properly. Not that he'd done it himself, but he'd heard stories. It made his heart ache for her.

"You're not eating?" she asked, with a sly smile that curled the edges of her lips. "I thought a big strong cowboy like yourself would devour that meal."

He glanced down at the thick and juicy piece of steak sitting on his plate. Along with the boiled potatoes and vegetables, it looked delicious. Suddenly, though, he'd lost his appetite. It had to be the way his mind was going—sending this woman back to whatever sent her packing was wrong on every level. Karl couldn't live with himself if he even contemplated it. Not to mention what might happen to his wife if she returned to whatever she was running from.

Sure, he'd been blissfully unaware of her existence until last night, but now he knew about her, Karl was reacting in a way he'd never done before. Not with any female. He wasn't totally against getting to know Florence, or even staying married to her.

He almost choked at that thought.

Karl studied the demure woman sitting opposite him. She seemed innocent and was certainly not worldly. The fact she didn't want to talk about her problems bothered him, especially after what Floyd had endured trying to keep Kathryn, *his* proxy bride, safe from a pursuer. He fervently hoped his wife's situation wasn't along those lines. "Is another man pursuing you?" He'd blurted out the words before he could stop himself.

Her look of confusion told Karl he was completely off base. He shook his head then. "Forget I said anything. My brother's proxy bride brought a whole heap of trouble with her." The more he opened his mouth, the deeper he found himself entrenched in something he didn't want to explain.

"I'm not in any trouble," she said, suddenly lifting her chin in defiance. "If you really must know, my drunken father told his drinking buddies, who happened to be his cowpokes, I was available for one of them to claim." She shuddered and his heart broke. "I was being harassed by no-good cowboys. One in particular decided I'd make a good wife for him. Cheaper than a whore." She glanced down at her hands and licked her lips before speaking again. "He was in the lockup when I left town. Not even the sheriff knows where I was headed, so Hank doesn't know where I've gone."

He watched as she fought back her emotions. Karl couldn't even imagine what Florence had been through. She reached out and picked up the mug of tea sitting in front of her, hands shaking. Taking dainty sips, she glanced over the top of the mug at him. "So what now? I get a room at the hotel, and then what?"

Indeed, then what? Karl's heart thudded. He couldn't do this, couldn't send her packing, back to danger, or goodness knew what. "I'm not putting you up in the hotel," he said, but before he could finish, he noticed her shocked expression.

"I have no money," she whispered.

"You're coming home with me." Karl's words were firm, as though he'd finally come to a decision. The tears that had been pooling in her eyes suddenly flooded her cheeks.

Chapter Two

Karl stood next to his wife as she collected up stores from the mercantile. He had next to nothing back in the cottage, and Florence promised she was a half decent cook. She'd had to provide for the handful of cowboys on her father's ranch; the one she'd had to flee.

He told her about the springhouse and the items she'd find there, and promised to take her to see it later that day if she was up to it.

She insisted she did not need clothes, but Karl wasn't convinced. She'd brought little more than a carpetbag with her, and he knew she'd left in a hurry. Instead of letting her change his mind, he helped her pick out clothes she could wear on the ranch, as well as a gown suitable for church.

"I don't need all these clothes," Florence insisted, but he added them to their other purchases anyway, then sent her off to choose her more *delicate* requirements. Elizabeth Dalton, whose husband owned the mercantile, accompanied her.

Given what he knew now, Karl was pleased he'd driven to town in the wagon. He'd had no intention of taking his bride home with him, and if he'd listened to his gut, he'd be in a heap of trouble with only his horse to get both of them home, along with his wife's meagre luggage and their stores from the mercantile.

"Is that everything now?" Albert Dalton asked, as he added all Karl's purchases to his accounting book. Karl had never had such a large account before, but he'd never bought proper food before. Like Floyd before he'd married, Karl lived on canned beans, bacon, and eggs. Most of which he got from the springhouse.

He opened his mouth to confirm that was it, when he spotted flowers out of the corner of his eye. He glanced over at his new bride. What a lovely surprise it would be for her to be given a bunch of flowers. At least, he thought it would be. He shook his head, then stepped toward them. Elizabeth smiled at him, then wrapped the flowers for him. Karl glanced over his shoulder; his wife had occupied herself with walking around the store, checking everything out. She had no idea what he was up to.

As he returned to the counter, he spotted Florence. She stood at the perfumed soap, and was breathing in their fragrance. "I'll take two of those, as well," he told Elizabeth quietly. Karl knew he was spoiling his wife, but it seemed she needed a little spoiling. How anyone could treat her so shabbily, he had no idea.

"It was lovely to meet you," Elizabeth told Florence as they left.

"And you," his wife answered. "They are lovely people," she told him as he helped her up onto the wagon, ready for their trip back to the ranch.

"They are," he said, then went to the back of the wagon to retrieve the two surprises he'd bought for her. He climbed up onto the wagon next to Florence and handed them over. "These are for you," he said, and was delighted by the look of surprise on her face.

"Oh, my goodness. Thank you, but you shouldn't have," she said, her voice full of joy. It was the first time he'd seen her truly smile, and it filled his heart with happiness.

"You're my wife; I'm allowed to spoil you." She spent much of the trip breathing in the fragrance of her wedding gifts, and Karl knew he'd done the right thing.

When they arrived at the entrance to the *Broken Arrow Ranch*, her eyes opened wide in surprise. Buildings were scattered around the property, indicating where each family lived. From their vantage point, they looked like dots on a map, but in reality were cottages of three bedrooms or more. The largest of them all was the main house where Jacob lived with his family, but even that large mansion looked small from here. Not that it surprised him—every time he sat here at the entrance, he was in awe of the size of the ranch. Thousands of acres stood in front of them.

"It's huge," Florence said breathlessly.

"It is. Although it's one big ranch, it's spread between three owners. Each of them manage their own acreage." As they drove through the property, Karl pointed out the various buildings to her. When they drove past the main house, he pointed out the springhouse. "I'll take you there when you're up to it," he said.

She suddenly appeared tired, and Karl wanted to get her home as quickly as possible. She'd had a long trip, and he should have been more considerate. "You look exhausted," he said quietly. "Perhaps a nap might help."

She blinked rapidly, as though fighting sleep. "I think that's a good idea. At least after I have unpacked this lot."

"I can do that."

"I'd rather do it myself. Then I'll know where everything is."

He nodded. She was right. If Karl unpacked the supplies, she wouldn't know where to find them. It shouldn't take too long, so he agreed. Of course, he would carry everything into the cottage. "We're here," he said as he brought the horses to a halt and pulled on the brake.

He watched as she gave the cottage the once-over. Then a slow smile appeared on her lips. "I love it," Florence said as she turned to him. "I think I'm going to like it here."

"I sure hope so," he said under his breath, then helped his wife down from the wagon. It would take some getting used to having a wife, and no longer living alone, but Karl saw how happy his brother Floyd was, and did want that same thing for himself.

Not to mention Florence. She deserved happiness in her life, and Karl was going to ensure she got it. As he opened the cottage door, he scooped her up and carried her across the threshold. His heart trembled at the absolute joy written all over her face.

Karl flicked back his wet hair and dried his face. He'd had a quick wash to prepare for supper—a *suggestion* from his new bride. The last thing he wanted was to give his wife a bad first impression. He was not one of those cowboys who never washed. He kept himself clean and tidy and wanted her to know that. He pulled his shirt back over his shoulders, leaving it unbuttoned as he always did at night.

Taking a deep breath, as if preparing for something terrible to happen, he headed to the kitchen, then sat down. Florence had set the table—not fancy like a restaurant or diner, but far more elaborate than he ever bothered with. She'd found a tablecloth somewhere. *In the pantry, perhaps?* He honestly didn't know. Karl couldn't recall ever using a tablecloth.

Old Charlie, who was the foreman when the brothers arrived at *Broken Arrow* after their father had died suddenly, previously occupied the cottage. Floyd and Karl had originally shared a cottage since there were no others available, but after Old Charlie passed on, it had been offered to Karl.

That must be it—the tablecloth had probably belonged to Old Charlie. Boy, that was a long time ago.

He glanced up to see Florence on the other side of the table, hands on her hips, and an expression that said she was ready to battle. *Did she really have a feisty temper?* He fervently hoped he wasn't about to see it now.

"Karl Adams," she said between gritted teeth. "Bare chests are not acceptable at my table." She had a frown that was enough to send the bravest of men running.

"I, um…" What could he say? She obviously had standards, and he did not. He stood then and buttoned his shirt. "Sorry Ma'am." He sheepishly looked away.

"Don't you Ma'am me," she said firmly as she looked him up and down. "My name is Florence, but most folks call me Florrie. Now sit yourself down so I can serve up supper while it's still hot."

She looked far more refreshed since she'd napped. Karl was surprised at the amount of time she'd slept, but he knew he shouldn't have. Nearly two hours, but she'd traveled for days. That was enough to take it out of the strongest person, and she appeared quite frail at times. Probably because of her situation and the anxiety it has caused her. Karl hoped that would soon change.

As he sat back at the table, she placed a large serving of chicken pie with vegetables in front of him. Karl leaned in and breathed in the aroma. It smelled delicious. He had been spoiled since Kathryn, Floyd's wife, had arrived, being invited for supper at least twice a week. But now he had his own built-in cook. A man could get very used to that.

"How did you have time to make this?" Not that he was complaining. Karl was sure it would taste as good as it smelled.

She shrugged her shoulders. "I'm used to cooking on the fly. Cooking for two is far easier than cooking for a handful of hungry cowboys."

She reached across the table as she sat down and clasped his hand. "Are you saying grace, or shall I do it?"

It had been so long since Karl had said grace at his own table, he hadn't given it a thought.

"You can do it." He said it as though he was handing her the keys to the kingdom. When what he was really doing was getting himself out of a tight spot. It had been so long now, he wasn't sure he could find the words.

"Thank you, Lord for this food, and a roof over our heads. Thanks also for sending me to a wonderful man. Amen."

"Amen."

Karl knew he hadn't proven himself as a good husband—yet—but was determined to do so. The coming days would show his true colors, one way or the other. As much as he believed himself to be a good person, it was up to Florrie to determine if his assessment of his character was correct.

The meal was delicious, as he knew it would be. Almost the moment he finished eating, his plate was scooped up from in front of him and replaced with a bowl of rice pudding. It was heavenly, and Karl didn't know what he'd done to deserve the angel sitting opposite him. The moment he got the chance, he would have to thank Floyd.

Not that his brother really deserved his thanks— he'd gone behind Karl's back to arrange a proxy bride, when he'd clearly told Floyd he wasn't interested. But all that bitterness had dropped away now that he'd met Florrie. He gazed across the table at her and wondered what their lives together would look like. She was used to living on a ranch, so that had to be a bonus. Many women, especially city gals, did not adapt to the lifestyle and the difficulties of living in the middle of nowhere, but Florrie was already used to it.

He hadn't breached the subject with her, deciding it was too soon, but did his wife want children? It was something Karl had thought about a lot over the years, but thought he'd never accomplish. Without a wife, children weren't part of the plan, and he'd decided God must have other plans for him. What those plans were, he hadn't figured out. Perhaps now he would learn the truth about His plans for Karl.

He stared at his wife's riot of red hair. Her curls went every which way, including across her face. He wanted to reach across and push them back behind her ears, but he dare not be so forward this early in their relationship. It got him to thinking—would their children have red hair, or would they have brown hair like their father?

Either way, he would be thrilled to one day become a father, should the Good Lord bless them in that way. His heart fluttered at the thought and filled him with more joy than Karl ever thought possible.

He shook himself mentally. It was far too soon to be thinking this way. He and Florrie hadn't even spent twelve hours together, let alone a night, and for all he knew, she may have decided she was not interested in having relations with him. If that happened, children were completely out of the picture. Suddenly, his heart thudded. Perhaps it was time for a heart-to-heart with his bride.

Florrie awoke to a tangle of legs and arms. She was still wrapped in Karl's arms and wasn't particularly concerned. She began to climb out of bed, then decided to stay instead, and glanced down into his face as he lay sleeping. Her husband was a handsome man—she'd noticed the moment they met. Even despite his obvious anguish when she first saw him at the stage office.

His hair flicked back over his forehead and she was sorely tempted to brush it away. Instead, she continued to study him, watching the changing emotions that filled his face. *Did everyone do this?* She assumed when a person slept, their faces relaxed, and no emotions were visible.

He stirred slightly, then groaned low. Unable to resist any longer, Florrie leaned in and kissed him on the lips. She knew she was being bold, but Karl had been nothing, but caring and gentle with her. He'd ensured her every need was met, and that she came to no harm. She'd never been treated so well in her life, and they'd been together less than a day. She wondered what the future would bring for the pair.

Without warning, two strong arms wrapped around her and pulled her close, reciprocating her kiss. Only his was not so gentle; it was far more urgent. He shoved her curls back behind her ears and found a path for his lips. Warmth flooded Florrie as his arms surrounded her. Her heart fluttered, and she knew her life had changed for the better.

Suddenly, Karl flipped her beneath himself and stared down at her, grinning. Little did she know when she became a proxy bride, her life would be changed forever.

"Don't you have to work?" She stared up at him and into his beautiful blue eyes. She'd never seen eyes so blue, except in the sky in the summertime. A slow smile curved on his face, and instead of answering, he leaned in and kissed her again.

"Nope," he said when he came up for air. "My boss gave me a few days off for our honeymoon."

Florrie figured that was a good thing. They could get to know each other better before he had to go back to work and leave her alone at the cottage. She didn't know anyone else, and the property was new to her. Should something happen, she'd have nowhere to go. Not that Florrie expected anything untoward to happen. No one, not her father, not even the sheriff knew where she'd gone. The sheriff only knew she'd taken the stage; she purposely didn't disclose her final destination. What he didn't know, he couldn't tell.

Not that she was afraid for her life. It wasn't like that, but from what little Karl had told her, Floyd's wife had been in a totally different situation. Florrie couldn't even begin to imagine how Kathryn must have felt. Sure, she'd run away, but she had no fear for her life, although she really didn't know what some of those cowboys back home were capable of, especially Hank. He could fly off the handle in a heartbeat.

She squeezed her eyes tightly closed. The last thing she wanted was to think about Idaho and what might have been. She was a married woman now, and in the arms of a man who had so far proven to be safe and loving. It's what she wanted, and what she needed. There was nothing more she could wish for, and silently prayed her thanks to God for sending her to heaven on earth.

Chapter Three

As they strolled hand in hand across the front paddock, Karl watched a flurry of expressions pass over his wife's face. She studied the surrounding scenery, something he took for granted. He was somewhat flummoxed as she lived on a ranch in Idaho, but from what she'd told him, it was far smaller. The way she'd explained her position on the ranch, she was nothing more than an unpaid servant for her father and a handful of cowboys.

How anyone could treat their own flesh and blood that way, he would never know. That said, he'd seen it time and again. His cousin Noah's wife, Mary, had been through something similar. Thank goodness she had been saved by Noah's enforced proxy marriage.

Despite his initial reluctance to continue his marriage with Florrie, he was now pleased for the unconventional way they'd got together. He was absolutely convinced Teddy, the family solicitor, had no inkling that Karl had not approved of their proxy marriage. It was difficult to think about where Florrie would be right now if he'd refused to follow through.

"Do you ever stay out overnight?" she almost whispered. He studied her and wondered if his wife was afraid to stay in the cottage alone.

"Occasionally, but it's rare. Of course there are cattle drives. We can be gone for days during those times." She nodded, and Karl was certain she knew all about that part of the business. "Your father's ranch has cattle?"

"Mostly. He has a few sheep too, and some milking cows, but the biggest part of his business is cattle. The rest are just a sideline. Of course, it's nothing like the size of this ranch." She flicked at the wildflowers in the paddock as she strolled along, then suddenly turned to him. "I might make a stew for tonight—if that's alright with you."

He reached for her hand and squeezed it. "I'll never refuse food of any sort."

She smiled then, and his heart filled with happiness. Floyd had tried to tell him what a difference a wife would make to his life, but Karl didn't listen. He knew, though, that he couldn't and shouldn't judge his marriage on one day of loving and good food. There was far more to a marriage, and he had so much to learn.

More than anything, Karl wanted to be a good husband. As the last man on the property to marry, he had a lot of good examples to follow, and if push came to shove, plenty of places to get advice.

They headed back to their cottage to allow Florrie plenty of time to prepare supper. There had been a number of times Karl had felt utter loneliness entering his humble home, but not today. This time was different; it felt like a real home, and not simply somewhere to eat and sleep. His wife had turned the hollow building into a home.

Almost the moment they arrived back, she poured him a coffee. "You sit and drink while I work." That didn't seem fair, but Florrie seemed fine with it. He enjoyed watching her move about the kitchen, watching her skirts swish around her legs, and loved the simple movement of her body. *Did that make him a terrible person? Admiring his wife for her physical attributes instead of her soul?*

He decided it didn't. They'd not known each other long enough yet to know the other. But Karl's aim was to get to know his wife completely, to understand her wants and needs, and to find out what he could do to give her the best life he could.

He planned to stay married to this woman, his wife, for a very long time, and the best way to ensure that happened was to get to know her. Really know her.

He stared at her over the rim of the mug as he sipped the hot beverage. "You make excellent coffee." She raised her eyebrows as though she totally didn't believe him. "It's true," he argued, though she hadn't said a word. "This is the best coffee I've had for ages."

"Perhaps then," she said seriously as she studied him. "Your coffee is mediocre, and mine is just that much better." She grinned, and then the grin turned into laughter. Karl couldn't help but join in. She turned her back on him then and began to cut up the meat and vegetables for the stew. The onions were already in the pan and sizzling, and he stood behind her, his arms going around her waist. Her warmth seeped into him, and Karl reveled in her closeness. Florrie leaned back into him and relaxed. "If I didn't have this stew to make, I'd…"

"You'd what," he whispered.

She turned her head and glanced back at him, a sly smile crossing his lips. "It doesn't matter, because I do have food to prepare."

He sighed then. "We could eat at the diner in town." He wiggled his eyebrows then, and she straightened up.

"Too late," she snapped. "Supper is more than half prepared. Perhaps we can go for a ride later? I'd like to see more of the property sometime." His arms slowly came down from around his wife. She was no fun, and was more concerned with making supper than anything right now. "When will I get to meet your brother and his wife?" She half turned her head as she said the words, and he almost groaned. He supposed he needed to introduce them, but Floyd deserved to wait after what he did. Not that Karl was complaining now—he was more than happy with his new wife, his proxy bride. He only hoped Florrie was happy with her end of the bargain.

With supper on cooking, the pair headed to the stables. As he tacked up his horse, Buddy, he watched Florrie do the same. He hadn't been convinced she knew how to ride, or even dress a horse—just because she lived on a ranch didn't mean she knew what she was doing. Karl was pleased to be proven wrong.

They led the horses out of the stables and headed toward the other cottages on the property. It would be helpful for Florrie to know the lay of the place in case of emergency. She would still have a pleasant view of the mountains from here. Perhaps some other time they could go further afield.

He pointed out the various cottages along the way, having already indicated Floyd and Kathryn's cottage, which was near to theirs. Chance and Laura weren't far away, and next was the main house. He would introduce his wife there on the way back, if there was still time.

"It's pretty out here," she said as she glanced about. "And the ranch is huge, but very isolated, too."

She was right—it was isolated here, and they quickly learned that lesson with the trouble that followed Floyd's wife. If they hadn't worked as a team, things could have turned out quite differently. Thank goodness it had all been fine in the end.

Karl knew his marriage would be a shock to most of the other cowboys. He'd been determined not to give in to the pressure of marrying. But that choice was taken out of his hands. He tensed at the thought, despite believing he'd resolved himself to the situation. "It takes some getting used to, but you're used to living on a ranch. I expect it won't be a problem for you?" He shrugged his shoulders then, assuming he was correct.

But what if he wasn't? Karl did not know the size of her father's ranch. With a handful of cowboys, it surely had to be a reasonable size, but he really didn't know. Cowboys often came and went in a heartbeat if they were mistreated. No such problems on the *Broken Arrow Ranch.* Everyone here was like family. Most were blood-relations. All had been here for too many years to mention.

The wind whipped up and her rage of curls went this way and that. Karl longed to reach out and force them into place, but didn't want to appear to forward. He felt a strange pull toward this new wife of his, and had no idea why. They'd known each other for such a small amount of time, and he didn't want to scare her off. Although, in reality, she had nowhere else to go. That didn't mean Karl could or should take advantage of the situation. He was brought up to be a gentleman, had lived his life that way, and would continue to behave in an exemplary manner.

Florrie gazed at him as though she saw right through him, and Karl shivered. Then suddenly she grinned. Tightly grabbing the reins, she took off, leaving him to follow in her wake. *So that was the game she wanted to play?* He quietly chuckled. Karl decided that meant she really did know how to ride. However, she didn't know Rosie, her horse, or what she was capable of, and that was a concern. Buddy could easily keep up, but Karl kept him slightly behind, ensuring he didn't get in Florrie's way, whatever she had planned.

Without warning, Rosie suddenly reared up, and Karl's heart thudded. His wife was in danger of being thrown. She held tight to Rosie's neck, and leaned in, whispering to the mare, reassuring her, until Rosie calmed down.

"What happened?" Karl was almost frantic, and his voice expressed his concern.

"Snake. I saw it out of the corner of my eye, but it was too late."

He glanced around, but there was no sign of it. Hopefully, the offending creature had slivered away, never to be seen again, but he doubted they were so lucky. "Do you want to return home?" He wouldn't blame her if she did, but Karl was enjoying his wife's company, and getting to know her better away from the cottage, where she insisted on cooking and cleaning, and acting like a servant. They were not fun things, and he wanted her to stop those activities and concentrate on him.

His errant thoughts stopped Karl in his tracks. *Was that really how he felt? Was he jealous that Florrie hadn't given him her full attention?* He sounded like a spoiled child, and that wouldn't do. He shook his head as if admonishing himself. He really needed to do better. Since she'd arrived, Florrie had done little in the way of fun things, except for now. She seemed to revel in riding and exploring. Unfortunately, he would have to return to work soon, so their time together was numbered.

As much as he didn't want her here to begin with, his bride was growing on him.

She didn't answer, so Karl decided for her. "We should probably return to the cottage. I'll introduce you to Jacob and Clarissa on our way home."

Clarissa opened the door and ushered them inside. "So nice to meet you, Florence."

"She prefers Florrie," Karl said, and his wife smiled.

"Florence is so formal, and my full name was always used to admonish me. I guess I came to hate it." She suddenly bit her lip as though she'd said far more than intended.

Karl's heart thudded. He was not aware of that, but he should have realized. Her father was a drunk who was willing to barter his daughter to whichever cowboy claimed her first. Of course, she would continue to work for him, for free, Karl was certain. The old man wouldn't want to lose his cook just because he married her off.

It made him wonder if that was the reason she was offered to whichever cowboy wanted her the most. That way, he wouldn't have to support her, but still got her services for free. He shook his head. *What a piece of work her father must be.*

"I'll organize a get-together soon," Clarissa said, and Florrie went pale. "Nothing to worry about," she said soothingly. "We're all family here." She indicated for them to sit down, and so they did. Florrie seemed far more nervous than he expected.

Karl jumped up as Jacob entered the room. "My cousin, Jacob," he said, glancing in his wife's direction. "And this is Florrie, my wife," he said, introducing her.

She glanced from one to the other. "I can see the resemblance."

Karl studied his cousin then. He couldn't see much of a resemblance, but it wasn't the first time they'd been compared. The two men circled each other.

"Nope. No resemblance at all." Karl grinned as he said the words, then took his seat next to his bride once more.

"I'll arrange a dinner," Clarissa told Jacob. "For Florrie to meet everyone." She turned to Florrie then. "The last thing we want is for you to feel isolated. We are all family here, even if we're not all blood relatives."

It warmed Karl's heart they had made his wife feel so welcome. Not that he'd ever had any doubt. That wasn't the way it worked on *Broken Arrow*. Everyone was welcome. He watched as Florrie glanced around. The main house was something special. As much as Jacob protested when anyone called his home a mansion, that's exactly what it was. The house had originally belonged to his great-grandfather, and he had spared no expense. The original fittings, including intricate chandeliers, still hung in every room. The woodstove was the original, and the furniture they sat on had been lovingly restored. The entire house was a lesson in history.

As much as Karl loved this house, he always felt in awe of it. Sure, it was his cousin's house, but it was far more than that. He had been so grateful when Barnabas, his uncle, had taken him and Floyd in when their own father had died suddenly. Neither of them wanted to leave their father's home, but the bank claimed it, and they had nowhere else to go.

Uncle Barnabas had taken them in and had them trained up. Two unwieldy teenagers in mourning, and not interested in becoming cowboys like their cousins. In hindsight, they were destined for this life, and were both now incredibly grateful. To have their own children grow up on the *Broken Arrow Ranch* was such a privilege, and he would be eternally grateful for the opportunity given to them at such a young age.

Clarissa and Florrie chatted while the men talked about ranch business. They were interrupted by the shouting of young Barnabas. "Someone is awake from his nap," Clarissa said, then left the room to collect their son.

"We should leave you to it," Karl said, standing.

Jacob stared at him momentarily, then glanced at Florrie. "Do you have another minute or two to spare? I'm sure Florrie would like to meet our boy."

Her face lit up at his words, and Karl didn't have the heart to take her away. "I would," she said before he could utter another word. Her expression had changed the moment Clarissa mentioned Barnabas, and he knew she was a softy for children. Karl wondered if she felt the same about having children of her own or whether her emotions were only for other people's children. Either way, it was something for them to deal with down the track. Not that the choice would be in either of their hands. That was something for the Almighty to decide, not mere mortals like Florrie or himself.

"Oh, he is absolutely adorable!" Florrie was on her feet and gazed at Barnabas as he ran across the room toward his father. The moment he reached Jacob, he grasped his father's trousers to hide from this person he didn't know.

Karl watched his wife as she continued to stare at the small boy. His heart fluttered. How he longed for a child with Florrie—should they be so blessed.

Jacob reached down and picked his son up. Barnabas glanced around the room, his eyes locking on the stranger in his midst. He reached out an arm toward Florrie, then suddenly tucked his head into his father's shoulder. Karl moved toward Florrie and put an arm around her.

"He's not always good with strangers, but he'll get used to you." Jacob's words seemed to put her at ease.

"We should go," Karl suddenly said. "We've taken up enough of your time." Besides, he wanted to spend more alone time with his wife, and the day was running away from them.

"It was lovely to meet you," Clarissa said, stepping toward Florrie, then pulled her into a hug. "I'll let you know about the dinner."

As the door closed behind them, Karl snatched up Florrie's hand. It felt soft and warm, and sent a shiver through him every time he touched her. It made him wonder if she felt the same. He glanced into her face, but there was no sign of any such thing. *Was this attraction one-sided?* He hoped not, because he didn't want her to be here against her will. Although that didn't appear to be the case.

Florrie had traveled here under her own steam and hadn't been forced to come. Well, that wasn't entirely true. She was coerced in that she had to get away from her father and his deceitful plans. That a daughter should feel she had to flee her home was appalling. The man ought to be ashamed of himself, but Karl was convinced that wasn't the case.

Otherwise, he wouldn't have made such an arrangement to begin with.

"I like your cousin and his wife," she suddenly said as she glanced back at the main house. "They have a beautiful home. I adore all the historical fittings they have there."

"It is beautiful. My father inherited a part of the property here, but sold his share to his brother. Ranching wasn't in his blood, and he went into business instead. Unfortunately, things went downhill quickly and by the time he died, there wasn't enough money to save the business or our home."

It was a time he'd prefer to forget, but Karl owed her an explanation. At least, he thought he did. Florrie didn't ask, but she surely wondered about the circumstances that brought Floyd and himself to this remote property.

The moment he opened the front door to their cottage, the aroma of the cooking food hit him. "That smells divine." He breathed in, delighting in this new situation he found himself in. Previously envious of his brother, he now reveled being in a similar position.

"I had a great time today," Florrie said over her shoulder as she stirred the stew.

His heart fluttered. Karl had enjoyed their day together as well. "You enjoyed meeting young Barnabas too, I could tell." He grinned at her then, but Florrie said nothing. He thought at the least she might tell him she loved children. But her silence led him to think perhaps she only liked other people's children.

"I did," she said as she moved away from the stove and pulled together ingredients—flour, butter, and milk. He watched as she molded the ingredients into what appeared to be a pastry of some sort, then formed the mixture into balls.

His curiosity got the better of him, and he couldn't resist any longer. "What are you making?"

She laughed then, and the sweet sound of her joy had his heart fluttering once more. "Dumplings. You must have had them sometime?"

He frowned then. "Can't say that I have." This wife of his was spoiling him, and not in a bad way. He looked forward to every moment spent with her and savored every bite of the food she made. It seemed to Karl she did an awful lot for him, but what had he done for her? Not a thing except to give her a roof over her head. Floyd had arranged for her to come here, had paid for her ticket, and even paid all her expenses along the way.

If it was the last thing he did, Karl would ensure he paid back every cent to his brother. Along with thanking Floyd for changing his life for the better.

Chapter Four

"I'm sorry," Karl said, as he donned his hat on his way out the door.

Florrie was by his side and wrapped her arms around him. She felt a shiver run down her spine as her hands connected with his body. Not that they were skin-on-skin, but his shirt was on the thin side, and he might as well wear no shirt. She would make a note to discard that one. "Of course you have to go back to work. I didn't expect you to stay away this long."

Karl's arm came up around her, and she reveled in his closeness. She knew she would miss him terribly, but he had to work. She had been incredibly lucky, ending up with a man with such high morals and a good work ethic. She'd seen many cowboys come and go on her father's ranch who put out their hand for their pay packet each week, but were incredibly lazy. Karl wasn't like that.

She suddenly felt empty as his arm came down. He lifted the other hand and nodded. "Thanks for this. The others will be envious." She'd packed him a lunch that included sandwiches made with leftover chicken, as well as biscuits she'd made earlier this morning. Karl hadn't said as much, but she'd guessed he skipped both breakfast and lunch before she'd arrived. It seemed even supper was a grim affair. How he'd worked all day on an empty stomach she'd never know.

At her father's ranch, she cooked breakfast and provided a packed lunch for each man. She also supplied a hot two-course meal every night. It was her father's way of trying to keep his men, but when you were underpaid and treated poorly, it would never appease them for long. Only a few stayed for any length of the time, and they were the worst of the bunch. The rest, the decent workers, usually left within the month. Often far earlier. Not that Florrie blamed them.

She watched as her husband walked across the paddock toward the barn. Two other men were not far behind him. They had to be Floyd and Chance. Clarissa's family dinner wasn't far off, and she would get to meet everyone then. The thought took her breath away. She'd never worried much about meeting new people on her father's ranch—most were there for such a short time. But this was different—she planned to stay here for the rest of her life. Provided Karl was here and provided he wanted her by his side. Where Karl went, Florrie would follow. She was his wife, after all.

She had certainly lucked out with Karl. When she'd learned of her father's plans for her, she knew she would have to take drastic action, but how? Florrie knew a time would come when she would have to escape his clutches. Under her father's eagle eye, there was little chance to meet men. The only time she left the ranch was when she drove into town to get supplies from the mercantile and pick up their mail from the post office. Thankfully, the latter was her responsibility, otherwise she would never have managed the proxy marriage without her father's knowledge.

A sign in the post office had alerted her to the idea. Once planted, she couldn't get it out of her head, and Florrie applied. Within two weeks, she was married and planning her get away.

"Hello!" She glanced toward Floyd's cottage at the sound. This had to be Floyd's wife, Kathryn. Karl had told her all about the trouble that had followed her to the *Broken Arrow Ranch*. It made Florrie's trouble blend into oblivion and she felt guilty about believing she had been hard done by.

"Hello!" she called back.

"Come on over." Kathryn indicated for her to visit, and despite feeling somewhat apprehensive, she pulled off her apron and headed toward the other cottage.

"Welcome," Kathryn said as she wrapped Florrie in a big hug. "You can't imagine how happy I am to finally meet you."

"I'm pleased to meet you too," Florrie said. Despite her misgivings, she really was delighted to meet another ranch wife. "Thank you for helping get me here. I don't know what I would have done otherwise."

Kathryn waved a hand across in front of her. "Think nothing of it. Now come inside and I'll make tea. Or do you prefer coffee?"

Florrie followed her hostess inside and glanced about. The cottage was laid out in exactly the same way as Karl's cottage. No doubt they were all built at the same time, and from the same design. Her father only had bunk houses for the cowboys. He did not allow them to marry, but was making an exception to rid himself of his daughter. He'd even planned to have a small cottage built for her and her chosen husband, whoever that might turn out to be. The first drunk to put up his hand, she guessed. Hank was the one who seemed most interested. The thought made her shiver, and the memory of those times made her heart thud. She was grateful to be rid of her drunken father and his wicked ways.

"How are you finding *Broken Arrow*? And Karl?" She pulled down two mugs from an overhead cupboard. "I do hope you're settling in. Let me know if you need anything."

She already liked Kathryn. She seemed genuine and caring, which is exactly what Karl had told her. But Florrie did like to make her own decisions about people. "Everyone I've met so far has been lovely. Friendly." From what her husband had said, she didn't expect that to change.

"Please, sit down and make yourself at home." Florrie sat, and soon the pair were chatting as though they were old friends. They had so much in common, and she knew they were going to become close. Kathryn was the closest she'd ever had to a sister. It filled her heart with joy.

Florrie felt as much apprehension now as she'd felt boarding the stagecoach less than a week ago. As she and Karl reached the main house, her heart pounded. She still wasn't sure about this family get-together Clarissa had planned.

"Florrie, wait up." She turned and relaxed a little to see Kathryn bringing up the rear. Floyd was trying to keep up with their son Clyde, and Kathryn carried their young daughter. "How are you feeling?"

"Nervous," she said quickly, before she could stop herself.

"This is Floyd," she said, indicating her husband, who now held the small boy. "This is Florrie, your brother's wife." She said the words as she glanced at each man. *Was she trying to make them feel guilty?* "You should have introduced Florrie to us before this, Karl."

"I, um…"

"We introduced ourselves," she said pointedly. "We're already great friends." She reached over and pulled Florrie into a hug with her free arm.

"Are you going to stand out there chatting, or are you lot coming inside?" Jacob grinned as he spoke, and Florrie realized there was nothing malicious in his words. He held the door open for them to enter.

Voices drifted down the hallway and had Florrie faltering. *Exactly how many people were coming to this get-together?* Karl reached out and took her hand, squeezing it in reassurance. "It will be all right," he whispered, then reached an arm around her. "Everyone here is family."

"And friendly," Kathryn added.

Florrie glanced across at her new friend and smiled tentatively. Kathryn had been in the exact same situation when she arrived. They'd talked about it that first day, and she'd been reassured by her new sister-in-law. But believing it would be all right, and living it, were two totally different things.

"Aunty!" Florrie was almost knocked off her feet by a young girl who wrapped herself around Florrie's middle. She glanced down at the sweet face and felt suddenly at ease. "You have pretty hair," the child said as she reached up to touch it.

"Hello," she said, squatting down to the girl's level. "What is your name?" She tried to keep her nerves under control, and the sweet child was helping.

"I'm Mabel." The little girl then skipped away and found a couple who were presumably her parents. "Your dress is pretty too," she threw back over her shoulder.

"What a sweetheart," Florrie declared as Karl led her into the large sitting room where everyone had assembled.

"Everyone, this is Florrie, my wife," Karl announced. "You know Jacob and Clarissa, this is Noah and his wife Mary…" All the names seemed to roll into one, and she didn't have a hope in Hades of remembering even half of them.

"You realize I won't remember your names, don't you?" She half laughed as she made the announcement. "I'm terrible at names, but I'll learn, eventually."

"I'm Mabel," the little girl piped up. "You won't forget my name, will you, Aunty?" Florrie had to fight back a grin.

"I promise, I won't. You are far too unforgettable," she said, bending down to place a kiss on the sweet girl's cheek. Before she knew what was happening, Florrie found herself gripped in a big hug, and almost knocked off balance. Karl grabbed her arm to stop her from falling.

"Mabel can get a little exuberant." The voice came out of nowhere. When she stood again, Mabel's mother stood in front of her. "I'm Abigail. Seth's wife and Mabel's aunt." She leaned in closer so only Florrie could hear. "She is like a daughter to us."

Florrie could do nothing but nod. No doubt she would learn the story behind Mabel living here at some point.

There were several children in the room, and adults watching them carefully. Until now, she hadn't noticed the large dining table in the next room. It was full to the brim with a variety of food. She slapped herself mentally. "I should have brought a contribution of some sort," she whispered.

"You're the guest of honor. You're not allowed to do that." Karl grinned at her, and she knew he was right.

Kathryn sidled up beside her and put an arm around her. "It's perfectly fine to feel overwhelmed," she said. "It's a lot to take in. Let me assure you, these are all good people. They'll look out for you."

Before long, Florrie felt as though she belonged here. As though she fit in and was wanted. It had been such a long time since she felt that way, and she had to force the tears back lest anyone see them.

Food was passed around the table, and Florrie couldn't help but enjoy the cheerful banter that continued throughout the meal. She had never sat through such a happy meal before. This was unlike any family get-together she'd ever encountered. Not that she had attended many. It was only Florrie and her father. They'd lost her mother before her teenage years, and her aunts lived too far away to be of help. They were blissfully unaware of the life she was forced into.

Florrie was convinced if her mother had still been alive, her life would not have taken such a turn for the worse, forcing her to flee the only home she'd ever known. She closed her eyes momentarily. Wondering about the past was useless—it wouldn't change anything. She had Karl now, and that's what was important.

Karl squeezed her hand under the table and leaned in close. "Everything all right?" he whispered.

Florrie took a deep breath and glanced about. Karl sat next to her, and Kathryn sat on the other side. Good people surrounded her, and she was safe. Karl wouldn't let her come to any harm, and she was sure the others here would also have her back. She turned to her husband and smiled. "I'm perfectly fine. Thank you for asking."

"When's dessert?" Mabel's voice carried all the way across the large table, and low laughter rumbled throughout the room.

"Really, Mabel?" Abigail's exasperated voice closely followed.

Florrie was smitten with Mabel. She was her own person, and despite being outspoken, was very likeable. She couldn't help but wonder what the young girl would be like when she grew up. One thing she was certain of, Mabel would not refrain from speaking her mind. Sometimes she wished she were more like Mabel. Had she been, her father would not have tried to push her into an unwanted marriage. But then again, she would never have met her husband.

She silently studied him and couldn't help but stare. He was the most handsome man she'd ever met, and she'd known many a cowboy over the years. Most of them slovenly and lazy. Thankfully, Karl wasn't like that. From what she could see, no one on this ranch was lazy. *Broken Arrow Ranch* was productive and prosperous. Totally the opposite of her father's ranch.

"Yummy."

Florrie glanced up to see Mabel licking her lips and rubbing her belly. Someone had cleared away and replaced the main course with a variety of desserts. Guilt overwhelmed her. Florrie should have helped. These people were not her slaves. She glanced across at Kathryn, who seemed to understand her more than anyone else.

"Next time," she whispered. "Today you are the guest of honor."

She knew Kathryn was right, but it didn't appease her sense of guilt. She glanced across the table at the goodies that waited to be eaten. Apple pie, muffins, Cherry Cobbler, Rice Pudding, and so much more. Each of the wives must have baked for days to put on this amazing display of food. She couldn't imagine how much work it had been. And all because of her.

She suddenly stood. "Thank you, everyone, for making me feel so welcome." Florrie didn't know what came over her. She was not one for public announcements, and now she felt heat rise up her cheeks and sat down as abruptly and she'd stood.

"We are very pleased to have you," Jacob said. "And look forward to getting to know you better."

"Next time I'll supply some of the food," she said, still feeling guilty about not doing so today.

She felt Karl's gaze on her. "She's an excellent cook, too." His voice didn't waver even one bit. It made her feel proud.

"Right up your alley," Floyd added, and everyone laughed.

Florrie felt so at ease with these people, her new family. It almost brought her to tears.

"That went well," Karl said, rubbing his belly as they headed for home. "I think I might have over-indulged."

Florrie glanced at him and raised her eyebrows. "You only think?" The tinkle of her laughter warmed his very soul. "Perhaps we should take a stroll. To walk off the extra food you ate." She laughed again, and he wanted nothing more than to pull her close.

"You enjoyed yourself, I can tell." He'd studied her throughout the meal, and she seemed comfortable amongst the large number of strangers. He'd reassured her beforehand, but she'd still been incredibly nervous. Not that he blamed her. It was a lot to contend with, especially after such a short period. Even more so, after what she'd endured. But she needed to get to know the rest of the family. It could be very isolating out here. For the wives, anyway. It was far from town, and everyone was spread across the property. In some ways, it was good because they all had their privacy, but until you were used to it, the isolation could be devastating.

"About that stroll…"

Karl glanced about. It was still quite light, so it wouldn't hurt, provided they didn't go too far. The stream wasn't too far away, so they could go there. "Why not? There's a lovely spot not far from here. Did you want to grab your shawl?"

She shook her head.

The night was still warm, but it could get chilly near the water. On the other hand, they wouldn't be gone long. Besides, he was more than willing to warm his wife up should she feel the cold. He probably shouldn't tell her that, though.

They walked in silence for the short distance, Karl reveling in her closeness. "Your family," she said, glancing at him as they continued walking. "They're lovely. Now that I've met them, I don't know why I was so nervous."

He reached up and patted her hand. "I tried to tell you. It seems Kathryn did too."

"She did. But being told and finding out for yourself are two totally different things."

She was right, of course, but thankfully it all turned out for the best. "Well, here we are. We used to have family picnics near here, but not anymore. Not with all the children running about." He didn't add that perhaps one day they'd have children, too. When that happened, *if* it happened, he wouldn't want his children put in harm's way either.

"I can see why you wouldn't picnic here with little ones, but the property is expansive. There must be plenty of places you could use."

"There are. We often use the paddock where we cross to the main house. There's a magnificent view from there, and the ground is fairly solid." He didn't add that she would see for herself sometime. "With so many of us now, the picnics are few and far between these days, but the children love them, so we still hold them now and then."

She glanced across at him and seemed suddenly shy. It made Karl wonder what she was about to say. "Do you think we might have children one day?"

She kicked at the ground with the toe of her shoe as she asked the question.

Warmth filled him as he studied her. "I hope so," he said, as he pulled her close. "I sure hope so." He glanced at her belly and wondered if they might already have begun their family. Without thinking, his hand covered her belly.

She glanced down, and her expression was blank. Florrie gave little away, and he still didn't know if she wanted children or not, but the question she posed made him think she probably did. "I know babies are a lot of work, but they're worth it." She studied him as she said the words, and Karl was relieved. He figured that meant they had the same aspirations when it came to offspring. He tried to imagine himself as a father, but he simply couldn't. Perhaps if his wife found herself with child, things would be different, but right now, it was beyond him.

At least if they found themselves in that situation, there were plenty of people around to help them. Or should he say to help Florrie? He would still have to go to work; he couldn't stay home all day just because she was pregnant.

Karl shook himself mentally—he was getting well ahead of himself. It would be months before they even had an inkling if there was a baby on the way. Florrie lifted her face to the little sun that remained.

The breeze blew gently through her hair and brushed her face. She appeared more contented now than he'd seen her since she arrived. It sent tremors down his spine, and without thinking, he pulled his wife against him.

Why he'd resisted his brother's suggestion of a wife, he had no idea. Right now, it felt like the best thing he'd ever done in his life. But Karl knew the best thing he'd ever done was to move to *Broken Arrow Ranch*. Not that he or Floyd had been given a choice in the matter, but Uncle Barnabas had done what he felt was right for them.

He'd hated his uncle for forcing them to come here, and Floyd wasn't much better. It hadn't taken long for the teens to realize they'd been offered what turned out to be the best move of their young lives. Soon they were both being trained to work on the ranch. It wasn't as though they didn't know how to ride already—they spent a good portion of their time at the ranch—most weekends, and every school holiday. They often resented their time spent on the ranch, but being a sole parent, their father couldn't work and take care of his boys as well.

Her head against his chest, Florrie moaned softly, and the sound brought him back to reality. His mind was playing tricks with him lately, and Karl wondered if it was the possibility of a child of his own that was triggering all these memories. Some were good, but others not so much.

"We should probably head home," he whispered, his chin laying gently on Florrie's head. "It will be dark soon."

She stepped out of his arms and glanced up at him. "Thank you for bringing me here," she said quietly. "It's so peaceful, and I've enjoyed it."

Not that it wasn't quiet elsewhere on the property. The entire ranch was serene, except perhaps when they were trying to round up cattle. That noise could be completely overwhelming if you weren't used to it.

He hooked his arm through Florrie's and they headed home. Karl felt like he was suddenly shrouded in tranquility, and it felt good. How he'd survived without Florrie, Karl would never know. He only knew he never wanted to lose her. His heart thudded at the thought, but she was here, she was his wife, and she wasn't going anywhere.

Chapter Five

Two weeks later…

Florrie couldn't contain her excitement.

They were going into town for the dance. She hadn't attended a dance for… years. She wasn't quite a teenager the last time she attended one, and her father was the only male she'd ever danced with— he refused to allow any of the local lads to accompany her, so it was Pa or no one. Her mother was still alive then, and life was good. Florrie sighed. Those were good days.

She put on her best gown, the one she reserved for church. Jacob offered the buggy, and Karl was about to go and hitch it up, ready for their trip. "Before you go," she called from the bedroom.

"Could you help?" It was a beautiful gown, there was no doubt, but it was impossible for her to secure the buttons herself. Apart from the fact they were tiny, you'd have to be a contortionist for the wearer to reach them.

Karl turned to her and grinned. "It would be my pleasure," he said, and Florrie was certain it would be. Her back to him, her husband began to secure the buttons. It didn't take long before his fingers began to roam.

"Really, Karl?" she said when his lips connected with her neck.

He sighed. "You really are a spoil sport." He chuckled then, and she smiled. Never in her wildest dreams did she imagine she'd enjoy cheerful banter like this with her husband. Mostly because her future promised a drunken, overbearing husband, with not an iota of love in his heart.

After her mother passed on, her father started drinking; mild at first, a glass here and there. It wasn't until Hank came to the ranch after her mother died that Pa's drinking got out of hand. His drunken behavior made it even more difficult for her to cope. Soon it became the norm, and she had no choice but to accept it.

It wasn't until recently when her father promised her to Hank, that Florrie realized things had gone well beyond acceptable, and she needed to get herself out of that situation.

"I thought we were going to town?" she said jokingly. Karl lifted his lips from her shoulder and paused.

"That *was* the plan," he said, chuckling.

"I hope it's *still* the plan," she said firmly, raising her eyebrows at her husband. "Now, if you'll just finish securing those buttons…"

Karl did as instructed, then removed his hands looking quite defeated. Florrie laughed, and he headed toward the front door.

By the time they arrived in Halliwell, Florrie had calmed down. She was still excited and was certain she would remain that way throughout the evening, but her heart wasn't pounding the way it had done earlier. When she thought about it, her heart had gone into a flurry when Karl had begun securing her gown. And when his hands had roamed. They might not have been together long, but there was definitely chemistry between them. The notion made her smile.

"What are you thinking about?" Karl's voice cut into her thoughts and brought Florrie back to the present.

She turned to face him. "Nothing really. Just looking forward to the evening's activities." He reached across and covered her hand.

"I am too. I haven't attended a dance for years. It should be fun." Karl pulled the buggy into an area close by the church hall where the dance was being held. It was already quite full. "I'm glad we didn't leave it too late to arrive," he said. "There aren't many spots left already."

"There seems to be an awful lot of people here," Florrie said as the buggy came to a halt.

Karl climbed down and held her by the waist as he helped her down. A shudder went through Florrie at his touch. Her husband affected her more than she thought possible, and it made her wonder if he felt the same way. "They come from far and wide when there's a dance. It's a big deal for many. Especially those who live further out than we do."

She should have realized. It was like that back home. Well, it wasn't home anymore, and if Florrie had her way, she would never return to that evil place. Thinking about her father's ranch made her tremble.

"Are you all right?" Karl whispered. "You're shaking."

His words sent another shudder through her. "I was thinking about my father and his ranch." She shook her head then, trying to clear her thoughts. "I never want to go there again. Not for any reason." Karl studied her in the moonlight. "I'm fine, honestly. Let's go inside and have some fun." Her husband still didn't seem convinced. She reached out and pulled him closer, then kissed his cheek. "I promise." Florrie then pulled him toward the entrance to the hall where Karl purchased their tickets, and they hurried inside.

"Oh, it's beautiful," Florrie said as she glanced about. The hall was decorated especially for the dance. Karl had never seen it like this before and was in awe of its transformation.

The band was warming up, and he couldn't wait to get started. Not that he was a good dancer—he'd had little practice over the years. It was the thought of being so close to Florrie that had his heart racing. Looking back, he had no idea why he'd been against getting a proxy bride. Still, it would have been nice to have been able to decide for himself, and not have it taken out of his hands by his brother.

He knew Floyd had his best interests at heart, but Karl was still a little annoyed at him. That feeling, that frustration, he was certain would eventually dissipate. Especially now he'd gotten to know his bride better. "This is great," Florrie said, pulling him out of his wayward thoughts. "Let's find somewhere to sit until the music begins." She reached out and grabbed his hand, pulling Karl toward a cluster of chairs.

He let her lead him near the back of the hall, where they would be closer to the band. He might regret it later, but for now, it made his wife happy, and that was important to him. As he glanced about, Karl realized the hall was filling up. They'd arrived before the advertised starting time, and on checking his watch, now discovered it was time for the dance to begin. His heart skipped a beat at the anticipation of holding Florrie while they danced. It would be an unfamiliar experience for them both, and he wondered if she was as excited about it as he was.

"Good evening, ladies and gentlemen," the bandmaster shouted, endeavoring to be heard over the chatter. "Thank you all for attending. And now, we will begin…" Being so close to the band, Karl heard him count to three, and then the music began.

"May I have this dance?" he asked Florrie as he stood. He reveled in the way she giggled as though they were complete strangers and had only just met. Karl reached out and took her hand, and she blushed. Heat rushed through him as they touched, and he inwardly admonished himself. He had touched her in so many ways since their marriage, but rarely in public. This was a whole different scenario for them both.

The first dance of the evening was a waltz. "I'm not a good dancer. In fact, I haven't danced since I was around twelve years old." She seemed oddly embarrassed, and Karl brushed her concerns aside.

"I'm not much better. Uncle Barnabas had all us boys taught to dance, but none of us really took to it, much to his frustration." Florrie laughed, and the sound set his heart to racing.

"We'll struggle together, shall we?" They both laughed then, and it sent a shiver down his spine.

They stepped onto the dance floor, along with a handful of other couples. Karl held Florrie's hand and placed his other hand around her waist. She followed suit. "If we just glide along and pretend to dance, I don't think anyone will notice," he said as he grinned.

Florrie stood rigid, as though the notion terrified her. The music was loud and the rhythm hard to follow, but they glided across the floor together. There was still a large space between them, which Karl found frustrating, to say the least. The song ended, and Florrie began to make her way back to their seats.

In a matter of moments, the music began again.

Karl grabbed her hand and pulled her to him, then they headed to the dance floor again. This time, he tucked Florrie in as close as he could get her. She studied him, silently asking if he knew what he was doing. They were, after all, out in public.

He knew exactly what he was doing—he was trying to take their relationship to a new level. To date, they had been like two strangers prancing around each other in their home and anywhere else they happened to be. It wasn't as though they each disliked the other, and they didn't merely tolerate the other person. The truth of the matter was, they were strangers who were forced together. Both were victims of what Floyd intended as an act of kindness to them both. Although Karl secretly believed they had already become far more.

Florrie was still quite rigid against him, and Karl found it frustrating she could not relax. This was meant to be a fun night, not an evening of terror. He ran his hand up and down her back as though he were trying to comfort her. "Relax," he whispered. "I want you to enjoy yourself." She glanced up at him and smiled tentatively. *Did that mean he was breaking through the barriers she'd built around herself?* He certainly hoped so.

Before long, she was resting her head on his chest, and Karl felt far happier. It told him she was finally relaxing. It made him feel more comfortable, too. The music stopped but began again in a matter of moments. Florrie glanced up at him. "Shall we go again?" she asked. A shiver went through him just from the way she looked at him.

It was the first time he could recall where she looked at him like someone who really mattered to her. It made him feel good, and warmth flooded him. Just knowing she cared, not because he would support her, but because she felt something for him, warmed his heart.

The music stopped, and the bandmaster announced they would take a brief break. Supper was being served, so the pair made their way to the tables. "The food looks delicious," Florrie announced as she studied the offerings.

"I agree. Grab a plate of food, then we'll go back to our seats to eat."

Florrie had insisted on preparing a light supper before leaving home, and Karl was so glad she did. He was already more than a little peckish. He could only imagine what he would have been like otherwise.

They finished eating, and Karl returned their plates to the kitchen ladies, only to find his wife as white as a ghost. "What's happened? You're pale." He was panicking when she didn't answer. He reached out and took her hand, and she glanced up at him.

"I… I can feel eyes on me. Do you think Hank could have found me?"

"You said he was in jail when you left, and even the sheriff didn't know where you went." He pushed his chair close to hers and put an arm around Florrie, pulling her tight against him. "I can't imagine it's even possible. Can you see him?"

She lifted her head and stared into his eyes. "I didn't see him. I just thought... never mind. It's probably my imagination."

Karl was certain it must be. He couldn't see anyone out of place, not that he knew everyone at the dance, but surely this Hank person would stand out. And if he was here, which Karl thought was near-impossible, he would have made his presence known by now. He had no doubt about that.

Sheriff Dawson wandered nearby, and Karl called him over. After a discussion between the two men, much to Karl's relief, the sheriff, who knew everyone for miles around, checked both inside and outside, but found nothing. They were free to enjoy the rest of their evening.

The band returned to their instruments, and Karl pulled his wife onto the dance floor. He knew it would be their last dance, as Florrie could not relax. The situation put him on edge.

Was the fool here in Halliwell? And did Karl need to look out for him? Luckily, there was a rifle under the seat of the buggy, and he would use it if he needed to defend his wife.

Thankfully, the drive home was uneventful, and he put it down to an overactive imagination on Florrie's behalf. Of course, it could also be a case of overthinking. Karl couldn't see how the man could find her, given the circumstances in which she left.

He said a silent prayer that she was safe and would continue to be protected under his care.

Chapter Six

Florrie couldn't believe she'd already been here for the better part of three months. Thankfully, there had been no signs of Hank since the night of the dance. She put it down to nerves, knowing full well if he was around, he would try to claim her as his own.

She fluttered around the cottage, ensuring all her chores were done. The bed was stripped; the sheets washed and on the clothesline. She'd swept the kitchen, and a supper of thick vegetable soup was simmering on the stove.

The moment Karl arrived home from work, they would head to Halliwell. She needed fresh supplies from the mercantile, and he'd promised her lunch at the diner. Florrie was looking forward to it, more than she'd realized. Not only because it would be a meal she didn't have to cook, but the opportunity to spend quality time with her husband was priceless these days. When they first met, she had no idea how much she would miss him when he was gone.

Sundays were the best days—they went to church together, then after lunch with the family, they spent the rest of the day relaxing together. They often visited the stream she'd come to love so much. Sometimes, they even had a picnic there. Just the two of them. With Karl working only a half day on Saturdays, she enjoyed those days, too. Every moment she got to spend with her husband was a bonus she never thought possible.

Back at her father's ranch, when she was being pushed into an unwanted marriage, the thought of spending time with her drunken husband-to-be churned her stomach to the point where she would often dry retch. On a few occasions, she did actually vomit. Her stomach roiled at the mere thought of marrying Hank. What her father had been thinking, she would never know. You would think he'd want better for his only child. Then again, being a drunk himself didn't help her father's thought process.

She pounded the bread dough one last time before placing a clean kitchen cloth on it and setting it aside to rise. She would place it in the oven the moment they arrived home. Florrie stirred the soup, then removed her apron. She hurried to the bathroom and pulled the pins out of her hair. As she reached for her hairbrush, she heard the front door open. She quickly brushed her hair—she didn't want him to see her looking such a mess.

Her heart fluttered at the knowledge her husband was home. She hurried out to the sitting room, a smile on her face, knowing Karl would embrace her the moment he set eyes on her. It felt as though they were still newlyweds, but after this amount of time, they really weren't. Every day she fell even more in love with her husband, and he told her often, he felt the same.

Florrie stopped in her tracks as she entered the sitting room. Shock overwhelmed her at the sight she saw before her. It wasn't Karl who had entered the cottage, but Hank. How he'd found her, she would never know. She closed her eyes momentarily and shook her head. Surely this was an apparition, and she was in the middle of a nightmare. She pinched herself to prove she was awake.

She opened her eyes again, but he still stood there, drunk as ever. So drunk, in fact, she wondered how he even stood upright. She glanced past him and through the window. A horse stood there, clear for anyone to see. Her only hope was *someone*, who she had no clue, would see this was out of place.

She glanced down. As always, his twin colts sat proudly on his hips. There were no guns in the cottage, which meant she couldn't defend herself if Hank took it upon himself to shoot her. She'd never known him to actually shoot anyone, but he often let off steam by shooting at objects around him.

Florrie swallowed back her emotions. It wouldn't do to let Hank see she was scared. "What are you doing here, Hank?" Her voice was stern, formidable even. She had to let him know this was not all right.

He lifted a hand and pointed at her. "You weren't easy to find," he said, swaying as he spoke. "But I found you." He smirked then, and Florrie wanted to slap him, but didn't dare move any closer to the drunken fool.

"Yes, you did," she said, disgust in her voice. "Now go home."

"Your father promised you to me, so you have to marry me," he said, his voice slurred and one hand sliding toward his colt.

Was he going to kill her? Florrie took a deep breath and immediately felt light-headed. "I don't feel well, Hank. I need to sit down."

He didn't speak, but motioned for her to sit. No longer being upright, she felt a little better, but her nerves were shot to pieces. *Would help be forthcoming, or would she end up being forced to leave the home she'd quickly come to love? And the husband she was deeply in love with?*

"You need to know," she said, her voice now shaking. "I am already married."

"You're married? But your father promised you to me." For a moment there, Florrie thought he was about to collapse on the floor. She knew if she'd been still standing, she'd be in a heap already, and not because of Hank. Her head was still spinning, although not quite as much as earlier.

"Why don't you sit down? I can get you some coffee." All she needed to do now was make it to the kitchen and not faint on her way there.

He nodded, and she slowly stood. Instead of staying in the sitting room as she'd hoped, Hank followed her to the kitchen and sat down at the table. He watched her every move. Florrie reached up and pulled down two mugs, then poured them each a coffee, fighting back nausea the entire time.

"I'm hungry," he said, studying her. "What's cooking?"

Hank was always hungry. "It's vegetable soup, but I've only just put it on. It's still raw. I have some cake though," she said, turning to get the cake tin from the cupboard. That's when she heard it—the front door opened so slowly it was barely audible. In his drunken state, Hank would miss it, but her relief was palpable.

She saw the barrel of the rifle before the person at the end of it. "I'll cut you a slice," she said, trying to distract him.

"Make it a big one," he said, moments before the barrel plowed into his back.

"Put your hands on the table, and don't move a muscle, you lowdown scumbag. And don't for one moment think I won't shoot you. I will," Kathryn said, shoving the rifle harder into Hank's back.

The drunk complied.

What seemed like forever, but was only a matter of minutes at most, Chance, Floyd, and Karl all arrived, guns in hand. Florrie near collapsed into a chair. Hank was dis-armed and hog-tied, and Floyd relieved Kathryn of her firearm, then pulled her close.

Karl took Florrie in his arms and held her tight. "Are you all right?"

Her heart pounded, her stomach churned, and her head was still spinning, but she was unharmed, and that was the main thing. She suddenly pulled out of his arms and ran to the bathroom. She threw up all her breakfast, and then some. For a while there, she thought she'd never stop. Karl wet a facecloth and wiped her face. "Feel better?" he asked, pulling her close again.

She nodded, then everything went black.

Karl sat nervously on the side of the bed, waiting for Florrie to awaken. He still couldn't believe she'd fainted, right there in his arms. Not that he should be surprised; she'd suffered so much despair because of that fool, Hank. He was safely on his way to the jail in Halliwell now, and Florrie was tucked up in bed safe and sound.

He studied her as she slept. She looked different somehow, but he couldn't put his finger on it. As he stared, her eyes fluttered open. Karl reached out a hand and caressed her cheek. "How do you feel now?" Her face was pale. Not that he should be surprised. Between her vomiting and fainting, she was sure to be unwell.

She began to sit up, but quickly lay back down. "Still a little light-headed."

He stared at her. "Still? You've had this before?"

"Only this morning," she said, a frown on her face. "I think it was the shock at seeing Hank standing in the sitting room."

Her hand still trembled, and Karl wondered how long it would be before she was back to normal. "Jacob sent for the doctor. You need to stay in bed until he arrives."

His wife glared at him. She didn't seem at all pleased. "I need to get out of bed," she said, making yet another attempt to sit up, only to lay back again.

"I've made you some tea," Kathryn said, placing a mug of tea on the night table. "Just take small sips."

"Kathryn." Florrie reached out and took her hand. "How are *you* feeling?"

Karl still couldn't believe the bravery his sister-in-law had shown. If it hadn't been for her, Florrie could easily be dead now.

She waved a hand in front of her. "I'm fine. It's not the first time I've brandished a rifle. I would have shot the fool too," she said, her voice a little shaky.

Florrie stared at her momentarily. "You saved my life," she said, tears rolling down her cheeks. Kathryn leaned in and hugged her. "Thank you," Florrie whispered as the two women hugged.

"Any time," Kathryn replied, and hugged Florrie again.

"You're sure?" Karl's head was spinning. First, his wife is confronted by a madman, and now he was given this unexpected news. He sat down at the kitchen table. His legs felt like jelly, and he didn't trust himself to stand unaided.

"I'm positive." Doc Petersen stared at him. "Are you all right, Karl? You might be in shock after the earlier events."

"Perhaps I am," Karl said. "I thought you said…" He wasn't sure he could bring himself to say the words. "My wife is with child?" He shook his head—that couldn't be right, could it?

Doc Petersen laughed. "That's exactly what I said. The dizziness, the vomiting, they were all signs. My examination only proved what I had already guessed."

"So she should stay in bed?" Karl would ensure Florrie didn't lift another finger for her entire pregnancy.

"Heck no. She needs to carry on with her normal routine. Exercise, have fun. There is absolutely no reason for her to be bedridden." He shook his head as if Karl were clueless. Which he was. "Today she can rest if she feels so inclined. She's been through a lot. But tomorrow, back to normal." He snapped his medical bag closed and glanced at Karl once more. "And don't you go coddling her. Florrie doesn't seem the type of woman who would welcome that." He snatched up his bag and headed toward the door, and waved over his shoulder. Karl followed him out. "I'll see her again in about a month. Earlier if you have any concerns."

Kathryn was waiting outside, along with Clarissa and Laura. "What's the verdict?" Kathryn demanded. "Is she…?"

Karl could barely hold back his grin. "It's not for me to say. She's awake if you want to visit." The three women hurried into the cottage, eager to hear the news. Before he went back inside, he heard the squeals of his wife's visitors. It put a huge smile on his face.

A short time later, the three trailed out of the bedroom. "Congratulations," they all said, massive grins on their faces.

"She's exhausted," Clarissa said. "We'll see you both later."

And then they were gone. Karl strolled into the bedroom and sat down next to his wife again. He leaned in and kissed her cheek. "We're having a baby," he whispered. Then his voice rose. "We're having a baby!" He couldn't contain his joy any longer. Deep down, though, he wondered what sort of father he would make.

Six weeks later…

Despite Karl's protests, Florrie planned to ride Rosie after finishing all her chores. "But you're pregnant," he argued.

"I am, but I'm not an invalid. If I was still living on my father's ranch, I would work as though nothing had changed. Ranch wives continue to work as normal right up until giving birth. I don't see why I should be any different." She glared at Karl, and he finally gave up. He had quickly learned Florrie had her own opinions, and wouldn't back down unnecessarily.

"Well, only if I come with you. In case something happens," he conceded.

They both knew nothing would happen. She'd ridden alone many times since arriving at the *Broken Arrow Ranch*, but never went far. Kathryn frequently accompanied her when she could secure a sitter for the children. More often than not, that turned out to be Laura, but the other wives were also happy to accommodate. "Just because you're not with me doesn't mean I go alone," she said firmly.

That caused him to frown. "Who goes with you? It's the first I'm hearing of it."

Florrie almost laughed out loud. *Was his pride hurt at not being needed for this particular task?* "Kathryn usually comes with me." She adored being able to take leisurely rides around the property, but she was not irresponsible. Florrie knew the dangers of riding alone. Should the horse buck her for whatever reason, she needed to know help was available. Especially now that she was carrying Karl's baby.

"I would prefer you took the buggy," he said. "I am certain Jacob wouldn't mind."

She fussed about the kitchen, disinclined to look her husband in the eye right now. Florrie was getting more annoyed with each word he spoke. "We'll see," she said, as she filled his mug again. "Now drink your coffee. It's nearly time for you to leave for work."

She finished packing his lunch and slipped an extra muffin in the bag. Knowing Karl, he would eat his lunch muffin on the way to work, and then end up hungry for the rest of the day. She finished preparing the stew and placed it in the large pot.

"I'm done," he said a few minutes later, and stood to leave. He sidled up behind his wife and put his arms around her. "Don't be angry at me," he whispered. "I worry about you and the baby." She turned around in his arms, calmed by his words. He cared for her more than anyone ever had almost her entire life. "What was that?" he said, looking startled.

Florrie grinned. "It's our daughter, letting us know she's there."

Karl's smile was the biggest she'd ever seen. "Do you mean our son?" He chuckled then, and slid his hand down to his wife's growing belly. Suddenly, his expression turned serious. "This is why I worry about you riding. What happens if you come off your horse?"

She knew he was right, but Florrie was reluctant to give in. Her hand covered his on her belly, and she sighed. "You're right. I don't want to risk losing the baby, but I also don't want to be stuck inside for the rest of my confinement." It was a dilemma, and they both knew it. She glanced up into her husband's face. He looked as concerned now as he did the day Hank had forced his way into the cottage. "All right. Ask Jacob. I guess that's better than not getting any fresh air."

He leaned in and hugged her tight. "Thank you," he whispered. "That makes me feel far more comfortable. And now I need to head to work."

Florrie rested her head on his chest. If she had her way, Karl would never go to work. She knew that was selfish, but she wanted him with her all the time. They both knew that was impractical and spent every possible moment together when he wasn't working. It made her love her husband even more, knowing he was a hard worker and would be a responsible father.

His hands roamed up and down her back until, finally, he leaned in and kissed her forehead. "As much as I'd love to stay, I really must leave." Florrie tipped her head up to face him, and Karl leaned in, brushing her lips lightly.

He snatched up his jacket and hat, then left the cottage at breakneck speed. Florrie knew he was sorely tempted to stay and got out of there as quickly as possible before he changed his mind.

She had never loved anyone so much in her entire life.

Epilogue

Three years later…

Florrie sat on the blanket Karl had placed on the grass for her and the twins. He wasn't entirely comfortable with the situation, but reluctantly agreed. His wife was attending the family picnic, whether or not he was there. She'd told him so in no uncertain terms.

"Lillie, Francis," she said, reaching for the toddlers. "Sit down quietly and eat your cookies."

This was the very reason Karl had wanted to skip today's picnic, but even before he'd objected, he knew Florrie would want to attend. With so many children to manage these days, picnics were few and far between. Adding toddlers to the mix made it hard work, especially for their mother.

But it made her happy, and whatever made her happy made his heart sing. Karl watched as Francis finished his cookie, then suddenly jumped up, no doubt ready to take off running as he was apt to do. His father snatched him up in record time. "Now, Son," he said firmly. "Mama told you to sit quietly. If I put you back down, will you do that?"

"He barely understands a word you're saying, Karl," Florrie admonished him, and he stared into his son's face.

"You understand, don't you, Francis?" The boy tucked his head into his Papa's shoulder and snuggled in. Warmth flooded Karl. Having a family made a huge difference in his life. He had gone from a lonely cowboy who wasn't prepared to contemplate a wife to a man who was content with his life and couldn't wait to get home from work each night.

He'd convinced himself that God did not have a plan for him, but was proven wrong.

"Lillie, come here and let me clean you up." Florrie grabbed the toddler as she too took off. Twins were hard work, and even more difficult when they were out on an open paddock where they could run to their heart's content. Only they couldn't because their parents couldn't keep up.

"I can mind them, Aunty," Mabel said. She had grown into such a beautiful young girl, who still cared for everyone and loved to help.

"They're a handful, Mabel." Karl's niece immediately pouted. "But I would appreciate you helping me out. We can do it together." She brightened up again at Florrie's words.

She glanced up at her husband. "I need to stand up," she said, reaching out to him. "My back is aching."

Not that he would say so, but they really should have stayed home. With another baby in her belly, the hard ground was not the easiest place for his wife to sit. Especially with little ones running about.

With Mabel taking charge of Lillie, and doing a fine job of it, he helped Florrie to her feet. "Let me get you a chair." He knew what the answer would be before he'd even uttered the words.

"I'm fine. I just need to walk around for a while." He slipped his arm through hers, and they began to walk about with young Francis still asleep on his shoulder. Karl glanced at the vision before him. He had believed the twins would be the last of the babies on the *Broken Arrow Ranch*, but it had set off another round of babies. The wives all got clucky every time another baby was born, and they wanted more for themselves.

Right now, three of the wives were pregnant, all at different stages. Karl couldn't be happier—this was the perfect place to bring up a family. A whole new generation of cowboys, and maybe even a few cowgirls, were being raised. They would have the best lives possible, he knew.

Glancing across to where Florrie was sitting just moments ago, Lillie had her head on Mabel's lap, and was sound asleep like her brother, her flaming red hair spread out across the young girl's legs.

Everyone assembled there was happy and smiling, and there was more food than they could collectively eat in a week. The babies and toddlers outnumbered the parents, and it made him chuckle. What a wonderful place to grow up. Although he'd arrived in his teenage years, it had been a life-changing move.

The *Broken Arrow Ranch* was like a little town, except everyone who lived there was either family, or as close to family as you could get.

Kathryn came over to talk to them. "Everything all right?" She studied Florrie, who nodded her assent. "Picnic's over," she announced, much to Karl's confusion.

"Wh..what? Why?" He turned to Florrie. "Are you not okay?" Then he stared into her face and realized it was contorted in pain.

"Someone get Doc Petersen," Kathryn commanded, then directed Karl and Florrie toward their cottage. Mary took young Francis from his father, and Mabel continued to supervise Lillie. "Your wife is in labor," she told Karl.

He studied Florrie. "Why didn't you tell me?" Inwardly, he knew—she didn't want to spoil everyone's fun. "The baby isn't due yet," he told Kathryn. "It's too early." He was beginning to panic, but when he thought about it, he knew it was only early by a matter of days.

"Please everyone, don't leave," Florrie said between contractions. "This is meant to be a fun day. I don't want to be the one to spoil it."

After reassurance from the adults, she settled down. Karl lifted his wife and carried her back to their home. He laid her gently on the bed, and sat down beside her, knowing full well he'd soon dismissed.

"Karl, I need you to put water on to boil. As much as you can. And collect all the clean towels you can find." He glanced down at his wife, then put his hand to her belly. That baby was jumping about and was ready to come out. He leaned in and kissed her forehead. "I love you more than life itself," he whispered, then left the room to carry out the task set to him.

Karl thought his wife's labor would never end; it seemed to go on forever. Doc Petersen arrived in record time and delivered a healthy baby boy. They named him Theodore after the Adams' family lawyer who had arranged their proxy marriage, as well as those of all the Adams' men. Without him, Karl's beautiful family would not be here. He would still be a lonely cowboy with no purpose to his life, and Florrie would be married to a drunken fool who only wanted her as a possession.

Henry was the boy's middle name, to honor his father who had missed so much of his sons' lives.

Karl hated that his wife had to go through so much for their children to be born, but they both wanted a large family. In fact, Jacob had already declared it was time for each of the worker's cottages to be expanded to accommodate all the children they were all producing.

Never did Karl think a few years ago that he would be in this position right now. He held Florrie's hand as he sat on the chair next to her bed and kissed her forehead as she drifted off to sleep. He gently took his new son from her arms and gazed down into his face. He had the face of an angel, one that looked just like his mother. Karl closed his eyes and said a silent prayer of thanks.

He then stood and carried the new addition to his family for everyone to see. He was filled with pride and happiness as he walked toward the low murmurs coming from outside the cottage.

Mabel held the hand of each twin, their eyes opened wide with wonder. "This is your new baby brother," he told the twins, squatting down to their level. His heart filled with pride as they leaned in and kissed their new brother.

From the Author

Thank you for reading *A Bride for Karl*! I hope you enjoyed Florence and Karl's story as much as I did. That brings the *Brides of Broken Arrow* series to an end. I truly hope you have enjoyed getting to know the men and women of *Broken Arrow Ranch* and they stay in your hearts for a very long time.

About the

Author

Multi-published, award-winning and bestselling author Cheryl Wright, former secretary, debt collector, account manager, writing coach, and shopping tour hostess, loves reading.

She writes both historical and contemporary western romance, as well as romantic suspense.

She lives in Melbourne, Australia, and is married with two adult children and has six grandchildren. When she's not writing, she can be found in her craft room making greeting cards.

Links

Website: *http://www.cheryl-wright.com/*

Blog: *http://romance-authors.com/*

Facebook Reader Group:
https://www.facebook.com/groups/cherylwrightauthor/

Join My Newsletter:

https://cheryl-wright.com/newsletter/

CPSIA information can be obtained
at www.ICGtesting.com
Printed in the USA
LVHW040354211222
735681LV00009B/520